Bedtime at the Swamp

By Kristyn Crow

Illustrated by Macky Pamintuan

HarperCollins Publishers

Manufactured in China.
All rights reserved. No part of this book may be used or reproduced in
any manner whatsoever without written permission except in the case of brief
quotations embodied in critical articles and reviews. For information address
HarperCollins Children's Books, a division of HarperCollins Publishers,
1350 Avenue of the Americas, New York, NY 10019.
www.harpercollinschildrens.com

Library of Congress Cataloging-in-Publication Data is available.
ISBN 978-0-06-083951-2 (trade bdg.)
ISBN 978-0-06-083952-9 (lib. bdg.)

Design by Rachel L. Schoenberg
2 3 4 5 6 7 8 9 10
❖
First Edition

For Garrett, Kyle, Emily, Riley, Anna, Liam, and Kathryn,
who know that moms are tougher than monsters
—K.C.

For Chris and Winter
—M.P.

I was sittin' by a swamp just hummin' a tune
with the fireflies dancin' 'neath the fat gold moon
when off in the distance was a splashin' sound,
so I stood on my tippy-toes and looked around.

I heard...

Splish splash
rumba-rumba
bim bam BOOM!

Splish splash
rumba-rumba
bim bam BOOM!

Well, my hands were a-shakin' and my heartbeat raced
as I leaped through the marshes and a MONSTER chased!
When it followed behind me in the sludgy slime,
it was rockin' and swayin' the entire time.

It went...

Splish splash
rumba-rumba
bim bam BOOM!

Splish splash
rumba-rumba
bim bam BOOM!

So I hid in the branches of a willow tree,
and I saw my kid sister staring up at me!
She said, "Ma said to fetch you 'cause it's time for bed!"
"But SIS! There's a monster in the swamp!" I said.

We heard…

Splish splash
rumba-rumba
bim bam BOOM!

Splish splash
rumba-rumba
bim bam BOOM!

Then OUT crept a shadow from the swampy place.
We were scared till we saw our older brother's face.
He said, "Ma said to fetch you 'cause it's time for bed!"
"QUICK! HIDE! There's a monster in the swamp!" we said.

We heard...

Splish splash
rumba-rumba
bim bam BOOM!

Splish splash
rumba-rumba
bim bam BOOM!

Well, we looked for the monster, wonderin' where he went,
till we spied our two cousins that our ma had sent,
sayin', "We came to fetch you 'cause it's time for bed!"
"WATCH OUT! There's a monster in the swamp!" we said.

We heard...

Splish splash
rumba-rumba
bim bam BOOM!

Splish splash
rumba-rumba
bim bam BOOM!

So we all sat and shivered 'neath the fat gold moon.

And the crickets were chirpin'
And the catfish were slurpin'
And the frogs were a-croakin'
And our feet were a-soakin'
And the tree was a-stoopin'
And my eyelids were droopin'

And we clung to each other full of dread and fear.
I said, "Hey, do you think we'll spend the night up here?"

Then we heard...

Splish splash
rumba-rumba
bim bam BOOM!

Splish splash
rumba-rumba
bim bam BOOM!

And OUT sprang the monster that had made us scared,
with its big feet a-stompin' and its sharp teeth bared.
I yelled, "HELP! It's the Creature from the Black Lagoon!"
But just when we thought we faced certain doom,

we heard…

Splish splash
rumba-rumba
bim bam BOOM!

Splish splash
rumba-rumba
bim bam BOOM!

Then OUT of the darkness stomped my dear ol' MA!
She burst through the cattails and she cried, "Ah-HA!
I've been tryin' to get you children home to bed,
and I find you a-hidin' in this tree instead!"

And we went...

Crunch crash
tumble-tumble
split splat SPLOOM!

Crunch crash
tumble-tumble
split splat SPLOOM!

Well, Ma looked us over, sayin', "No one's hurt,
but I don't think I've EVER seen so much dirt!
Now all of you, go and get washed up for bed!
And that goes for your new playmate, too," she said.

So he went...

Splish splash rumba-rumba bim bam BOOM!

And we went...

Splish splash rumba-rumba bim bam BOOM!

And I went…

Splish splash

rumba-rumba

Click!